Junkyard Dog

Monique Polak

ORCA BOOK PUBLISHERS

Orca currents

Library and Archives Canada Cataloguing in Publication

Polak, Monique

Junkyard dog / written by Monique Polak.

(Orca currents)

ISBN 978-1-55469-156-2 (bound).--ISBN 978-1-55469-155-5 (pbk.)

I. Title. II. Series: Orca currents

PS8631.O43J85 2009   jC813'.6   C2009-902828-X

Summary: At his new job taking care of guard dogs, Justin discovers that
the working dogs are being mistreated.

First published in the United States, 2009
Library of Congress Control Number: 2009928217

Orca Book Publishers gratefully acknowledges the support for its publishing
programs provided by the following agencies: the Government of Canada
through the Book Publishing Industry Development Program and the
Canada Council for the Arts, and the Province of British Columbia
through the BC Arts Council and the Book Publishing Tax Credit.

Cover design by Teresa Bubela
Cover photography by Getty Images
Author photo by Elena Clamen

Orca Book Publishers
PO Box 5626, Station B
Victoria, BC Canada
V8R 6S4

Orca Book Publishers
PO Box 468
Custer, WA USA
98240-0468

www.orcabook.com
Printed and bound in Canada.
Printed on 100% PCW recycled paper.
12 11 10 09 • 4 3 2 1

For Stephen Lighter,
irresistible mischief-maker.

chapter one

Everyone else just calls him Dog. I call him
Smokey. Not out loud, of course. Customers
aren't supposed to talk to him. He's a
German shepherd. He's mostly black with
some tan. His muzzle is the color of smoke.
There are matted clumps on his back coat.
He looks like he needs a good brushing.

The sales clerk doesn't bother saying
"hi" or "what can I get you?" His name
is Pete. It says so in curly letters on his
shirt pocket. Pete knows I never buy the

stuff other people come in here for—soft drinks, cigarettes, a dozen eggs. I don't shop in convenience stores. There's no way I'd spend two bucks on a carton of milk. I only come in to drop off empties.

And to see Smokey.

I have a shopping cart, the kind old people use for groceries. I found it on the curb by our apartment. One wheel wobbles, so the cart lists a little to the right, but it's still good for hauling empties. Today, my cart is loaded with plastic bags, each one overflowing with empties.

Pete leans over the counter to grab the bags. From the way he uses only his fingertips, you'd think he was afraid of catching cooties. That bothers me. I may not be dressed fancy, in a blue blazer like the prep-school boys, but I don't have cooties. Of course, I don't say anything. I need Pete.

The beer bottles make a clinking noise. There are sixty-six of them and two dozen plastic soft-drink bottles in all. Monday is recycling day, and you'd be surprised how many people put refundable bottles in their blue boxes. It helps, too, that people party on the weekend. Ten of those beer bottles are Dad's. And that was just Friday night.

"One, two..." Pete always counts the bottles, even when I tell him how many there are. I figure he'd trust me by now, but he doesn't. I fiddle with my baseball cap, pulling it down so it covers more of my forehead.

Pete scoops up the last bag and heads for the metal basket where they keep empties. That's when I make my move.

First I take a quick look around to make sure no one's watching.

No one is.

I have to be quick. Pete will only be busy for a couple of minutes.

I reach into the front pocket of my jeans. I wrapped the chunk of hamburger in plastic. I found the meat where I collect bottles in our apartment building—the garbage room downstairs, next to the garage.

I knew as soon as I smelled it that the meat was still good. I thought about Smokey straightaway. All he eats is kibble.

There's an economy-size bag of it behind the counter.

Smokey is lying on the floor underneath the cash register. His head is resting between his front legs, but I feel his sad brown eyes watching me. He is trying to decide if I mean trouble.

When I come closer, the hair on his neck stands up, and a low warning growl comes from deep in his chest. His lips curl, and I can see his teeth. They're old and yellow, and his gums look swollen. But his legs are strong and muscular.

I peel off the plastic and toss him the hamburger. His eyes follow the chunk of meat as it makes a quick arc in the air, then lands at his front paws. He looks at me again, then over at Pete, who is still rearranging bottles. Smokey gobbles down the piece of hamburger.

He lowers his head and gives me another look. I wish I had more hamburger.

The bell on the door jingles when Mrs. MacAlear, the old lady who lives in the apartment next to ours, comes in.

She nods when she sees me. Then she opens her purse and takes out a sheet of paper, waving it in the air like a flag.

"I understand you people have a photocopy machine in here. I need a copy, please," she says in a too-loud voice.

Pete looks up from the metal basket. "Machine's out of order."

Mrs. MacAlear marches up to the counter. "What's that you said? You ordered what?"

"I said the machine's out of order." Pete moves closer to Mrs. MacAlear and raises his voice. "We called the technician, but he still hasn't shown up."

"In my day," Mrs. MacAlear says, "that sort of thing didn't happen."

In her day, photocopy machines hadn't been invented.

Pete is back at the cash, counting out my money. "Seven dollars and eighty cents," he says without looking at me.

Mrs. MacAlear smiles when she spots Smokey. "Well hello, boy," she says as if they are old friends.

"Ma'am," Pete says. I notice he looks at

her when he speaks. "It's best not to talk to the dog."

"Why ever not? I used to have a German shepherd just like this one. Only mine was a little better groomed. Gustav. He was a fine—" She stops in midsentence. "Oh," she says, sliding the paper back into her purse, "I see."

Pete nods. "That's right. This here's a working dog."

For a second, Mrs. MacAlear shuts her eyes. I can't tell if it's because she feels bad for Smokey—or if she misses Gustav.

"Might you know of another place where I could make a photocopy?" Mrs. MacAlear asks. She takes another look at Smokey and shakes her head.

"There's an office supply store down the block." Then Pete looks over at me. "What are you still doing here, kid?" He says it like I'm a fly he wants to swat.

"Uh," I say, tucking the change into my back pocket, "I was just leaving."

I want to say bye to Smokey, but I know I can't. So I say so in my head—the way I say most things.

chapter two

I'm at the bathroom mirror, adjusting my baseball cap. If I tilt it a little to the right, but not too much, it covers all the bald spots. They've gotten worse lately. At first there was just thinning, but now there are a few spots the size of quarters where there's no hair at all. Those spots seem to be getting bigger. I try not to think about it, but it's hard. If I were a fifty-year-old guy going bald, it wouldn't be so bad, but I'm not even fourteen yet.

"Have you seen my bank card?" Dad calls from the other room.

"Nope, I haven't seen it."

Dad is not listening. He is rummaging through a drawer and swearing. "Where the hell is it?" I hear him throwing stuff. That jangling sound must be his keys. He must've just thrown them against the wall. My body bristles. I hate when Dad loses it.

When Dad storms by the bathroom, I'm still adjusting my cap. "That hair business is all her fault. Imagine a woman abandoning her kid like that. I mean, you're no angel, Justin. But still. It's no wonder you're going bald. Now where'd that damn card get to?"

Dad blames Mom for the trouble with my hair. I don't know if it's true, or if he just likes blaming her for stuff.

There, the spots are all covered. But Dad won't let me leave till I help him find the bank card. I hope this isn't going to make me late for school.

"Somebody could empty out my bank account," Dad mutters. I don't say what I am thinking: that somebody already has emptied out his account. Him. It takes a while, but in the end, I find the card under Dad's side of the pullout bed. The card is covered with dust bunnies.

Dad wipes the card clean. "You need to do a better job on the mopping," he says.

"Justin." Mrs. Thompson looks at me over the top of her reading glasses. "Did you get a late slip?"

"Um, ma'am, do I have to?"

Three late slips and they call your parents. Or in my case, my dad. Last time he made such a fuss the principal threw him out of the building.

"Let me tell you, Justin, I'm way smarter than that principal of yours," Dad said afterward. "You think he ever wrote a PhD thesis?" Dad did his PhD on Canadian history. Before I was born, he had a job teaching at the university, only it didn't last. Dad says it was because everyone in his department was an idiot. I figure it might have had something to do with Dad.

He doesn't like it when people disagree with him.

Mrs. Thompson gives me a tight-lipped smile. "All right then, Justin. But next time, you'll have to get a late slip. And take off that baseball cap. This isn't a ballpark."

I know from the way she's looking at me, her eyes practically burning a hole through my cap, there's no use objecting.

Most of the teachers know about my hair, so they let me wear my cap in class. But Mrs. Thompson is new.

I can feel my cheeks heating up. I take a deep breath and lift the cap off my head. There. I did it.

Someone snickers.

If only I could disappear right now.

"Ooh," a girl calls out. "Gross!"

Mrs. Thompson sucks in her cheeks, and for a second I feel sorry for her. She didn't know what she was getting into. "Now, now, Carleen," Mrs. Thompson says, her voice higher than usual. "Let's get back to our fractions."

I try to concentrate on the fractions

Mrs. Thompson is writing on the board, but it's hard.

I can't blame Carleen for calling out "Gross!" My head looks gross to me too.

I'm dividing ninety-six by three when Mrs. Thompson taps my shoulder. "You can put your cap back on if you'd like," she whispers.

I take the cap out of my desk and slip it on.

When I look back at my exercise book, I notice a yellow smiley-face sticker that wasn't there a minute ago. Where'd it come from? Not Mrs. Thompson. I'd have noticed if it was her.

I turn to my right. The girl sitting there is named Amanda Iverson. Amanda has green eyes and wavy red hair. She smells good, like vanilla cake. When she catches me looking at her, she smiles.

I point at the sticker on my book.

Amanda shrugs. But I spot the packet of smiley stickers under her math book. Maybe Amanda doesn't mind bald guys.

chapter three

I only have three empties that I found after school. It's not much of a haul. Pete will roll his eyes when I cash in three bottles. Dad will be disappointed I didn't bring home more money. But at least I get to see Smokey before I go back to the apartment.

The convenience store is crowded. Some private-school boys are at the counter, buying licorice and chocolate bars. One pulls a fifty-dollar bill out of his pocket.

"What's up, Dog?" another of the private-school boys calls out.

Pete doesn't say anything about not talking to Smokey.

"That's no dog," another boy says. He's shorter than the others. "That's a sorry excuse for an animal. He's older than my great-grampa."

His friends laugh. My shoulders tense up. They shouldn't be talking to Smokey like that.

The kid who paid with the fifty leans so far over the counter I can see the soles of his shoes. "Eat any crooks today?" he asks Smokey.

Even if Smokey doesn't understand the boys' words, he understands their tone. He knows they're being mean and that they're mocking him. But something tells me Pete isn't going to make them stop.

"Have any robbers with your kibble, you sorry excuse for an animal?" the kid asks.

His friends nudge each other and laugh some more.

From where I am, I can't see Smokey, but I hear him growl. It's a strange growl. Lower and more hoarse than you'd expect from a dog his size.

"Back off, will ya?" Pete finally says to the boy.

You go, Pete, I think, when something at the other end of the store—near the long row of freezers—comes crashing to the floor. The store window rattles.

I jump. Loud noises spook me. They remind me of what happens when Dad loses it.

Everyone turns to look—Pete, the private-school boys, me. Maybe it's a trick—a way to distract Pete and empty the cash when he isn't looking. Just because these kids are rich doesn't mean they're angels. I've seen them stuff bags of chips into their backpacks when Pete's back is turned.

"What the hell is going on back there?" Pete shouts.

There's no one by the freezers. On hot days, kids hang out there to cool off, but Popsicle weather's been over in Montreal for a couple of weeks now. I hear something rolling on the floor. It's a can of wax beans. My shoulders relax.

"Something must've fallen over," I call out.

A crate of bean cans has tumbled over. Some of the cans have come loose. I pick up the one in front of me.

"Dog!" I hear Pete say. "It's okay. Stay."

The noise must have upset Smokey too. After all, he's a guard dog.

One of the private-school boys grabs hold of his buddy's arm. "Let's get outta here," he says. "See the fangs on that monster? And the way his ears are sticking up?"

I don't like him calling Smokey a monster. If Smokey's baring his fangs, it's because he's on the alert.

I head for the cash. I feel like Smokey needs me. Like I understand him in a way no one else here does.

Another crate crashes to the floor. This one makes even more noise. But I'm less jumpy, because now at least I know where the sound is coming from. I hear shuffling behind the counter.

"Stay, Dog," Pete says. Smokey wants to get out. He wants to know what's happening at the back. It's what he's trained to do. Look for trouble.

The private-school boys rush out, blocking the entrance to the store. "I'll bet you anything that monster has rabies," one says.

"What I want to know," his friend says, "is why that dog doesn't bark. What good's a guard dog that can't bark?"

It's true. Smokey didn't bark. Now that I think of it, I've never heard him bark. Growl, yes, but not bark. Not once. It's weird how I never thought about it before.

I'm at the end of the aisle that leads to the cash register. I bend my head so I can see Smokey. The boys were right—his ears are sticking up, like he can hear something we can't.

"Don't get too close," Pete hisses.

But it's too late.

I'm too close. When Smokey bites my hand, it happens in slow motion. I see his sharp yellow fangs sink into the flesh between the bottom of my thumb and my pointer finger.

My hand hurts like crazy, and now there's blood on the tile floor.

But I'm not thinking about the blood or how much my hand hurts. I'm thinking about Smokey. If he wasn't upset, he'd never have bitten me. No way.

I crouch down. The guard hairs on Smokey's back are raised. I don't look him in the eye. Something tells me that would upset him again. Something also tells me Smokey's not angry. He's just scared.

"It's okay, Smokey," I say, extending my other hand.

"You all right, kid?" Pete sounds nervous— as if he's afraid he might lose his job. "Want me to call your mom or something?"

"I'm all right."

I reach out to stroke Smokey under his chin. It's the first time I've ever touched him. His fur feels good under my fingers.

I don't bother telling Pete I don't have a mom—or how if I do, I don't know where she's gone to.

Pete's relieved I don't want him to call anyone. I know, because he doesn't tell me to stop petting Smokey.

He's handing me Kleenex to stop the bleeding when someone else comes into the store.

"Thank god you're here!" Pete says. "Dog lost it just now. He bit this kid."

The man Pete is talking to is wearing navy blue coveralls. "How ya doing, kid?" he asks, leaning over to inspect my hand.

"It wasn't the dog's fault," I tell him. "There was a lot of noise and some kids were bugging him. I got too close."

"It doesn't look like he minds you being close right now," the man says. "Let me get in there and have a look at him."

The man works for the company that rents out dogs like Smokey. He takes hold of Smokey's muzzle and checks his eyes. "He's getting old is all. You sure you're okay, kid?"

I wrap the Kleenex tight around my hand so the bleeding stops. The dog guy has some antibiotic cream he wants me to use.

I feel him looking me up and down—a little like the way he looked at Smokey. "Seems to me you got a way with dogs. You know, we could use a kid like you when we do our rounds. It's mostly afternoons, but now and then we'd need you in the morning too. Early—before school starts. Any chance you might be interested in a part-time job?"

I lean on the counter to steady myself. "Interested? Sure, I'm interested. When can I start?"

chapter four

The van is waiting outside the school. When the door slides open, the first thing I notice is the smell of dog. "Get in!" a voice calls out, so I do—and the van takes off.

There are five huge animal crates in the back. When I peer through the gates, I see two liver-colored Dobermans, a square-jawed pit bull and a big shaggy black mutt.

The mutt charges against the bars of his crate and bares his teeth at me. What kind of job have I signed on for? "Nice to meet you too," I tell him.

"Titus," the driver says sternly. He keeps his eyes on the road. I can see his potbelly, but not his face. The black mutt settles down in his crate.

The guy from the convenience store is in the passenger seat. "I told you he'd be on time," he tells the driver.

He turns to me. "Kid, I don't think I introduced myself when we met last week. I'm Vince. This here's Floyd. You ready to learn the ropes?"

"Yup, I'm ready." What I'm really ready for is payday. Vince had said I'll get paid twenty dollars for every shift. It's less than minimum wage, but it means grocery money for Dad and me. It also means I may get to eat something besides mac and cheese this week. Maybe we'll get some hamburger—or even a couple of T-bone steaks—and I can keep the leftovers for Smokey.

"There isn't much to it," Vince says. "Basically you let the dogs out of the crates—you change their water, give 'em food and scoop the poop. There's a shovel on the floor."

The shovel is lodged between a crate and a tank of water.

When we hit a pothole, two of the crates crash into each other, and one of the Dobermans snarls. "So these dogs don't bark?" I say. Since Smokey bit me, I've been trying to imagine what it would feel like to be a dog who couldn't bark. I figure it'd be like having laryngitis—only worse, because laryngitis goes away.

"It's not that they don't bark," Vince says. "They can't bark. They're debarked. That way they can really scare the pants off a burglar."

"If they barked, we'd get grief from the people who live out by the junkyards where our dogs work," Floyd adds.

"How do you get a dog debarked?" I ask. "Does the vet do it?"

Floyd laughs. The weird thing is his laugh sounds like a dog's bark—hard and fast. We stop at a red light. Floyd turns to face me. He has a surprisingly thin face for a guy with such a big belly. A thin pale scar runs down from his forehead to the top of his nose. "Lemme give you some advice, kid," he says. He smiles, but not in a friendly way. "In this business, you don't wanna ask too many questions. It's better to just do as you're told."

I feel his eyes on me, waiting for me to say something. I think of the twenty bucks. One hundred bucks if I work five days a week. Vince said I might, if I'm a good worker. I might work more than that when they need me for morning shifts too. "Okay," I tell Floyd, "I get it. No more questions."

Our first stop is a used-car lot off the expressway. The brakes squeal as Floyd pulls into a narrow alley that leads to the back entrance. "Have a look at that baby!" Floyd says when we pass a shiny red convertible. "She's a 2006, maybe even a 2007—one hundred and seventy horsepower. Check out those chrome mags." When Floyd whistles, it sounds like a birdcall. "Can't you just see me driving that baby?"

"I don't think you'd fit behind the wheel," Vince says.

Floyd doesn't laugh—and neither do I. A guy like me doesn't mess with a guy like Floyd.

These are fancy cars all right—with sunroofs and tinted windows.

"That's the condo," Floyd says as he parks next to a small plywood shed. I always thought a condo was a fancy building with a doorman downstairs. This condo has no windows and looks out of place around all the fancy cars, like a weed at the botanical gardens.

"This is King and Killer's stop. They're the Dobies," Vince tells me.

Killer? I wonder how Killer got his name, but I remember what Floyd said about asking too many questions.

I take a deep breath as I pop open the back of the van. King and Killer must know where we are, because they're moving around inside their crates.

"Okay, boys," I say, my voice sounding braver than I feel, "time to get to work."

I catch a whiff of cigarette smoke. Vince and Floyd have gotten out of the van to have a smoke. "Hey, kid, don't forget your shovel!" Floyd calls out, laughing his bark-laugh.

I manage to slide the first crate to the back edge of the van. This would be way easier with Vince or Floyd's help, but it looks like I'm on my own. King—or is it Killer?—presses his muzzle against the bars.

I take another deep breath as I unlatch the crate. Please don't eat me, I think. Or if you do, do it fast and get it over with. But the Doberman doesn't eat me. Instead he leaps out of the crate. Most of his weight lands on his front legs. When he straightens himself out, he raises his head to sniff the air.

One more crate left. That's when I feel the heels of my sneakers slide into something gooey. Dog poop. I want to wipe it off my sneakers, but the other Doberman wants out of his crate. Now.

This must be Killer, I think when he bares his teeth. They're as sharp as razors.

"Everything okay back there, kid?" Vince calls out.

"Uh-huh." My fingers shake as I unlatch Killer's cage. I heard somewhere that dogs can smell fear. I wonder if Killer can smell mine. The latch makes a clicking sound. Killer leans back on his haunches, then sails right over my head. Who knew dogs could fly?

I grab the shovel. No wonder I stepped into a pile of poop—there's poop everywhere. Something tells me this place hasn't been shoveled in weeks. Now I understand why Vince wanted me to start work right away. "Where do you want me to dump all this?" I call out.

"Just add it to the pile by the shed," Vince calls back.

I work quickly and try to hold my breath. King and Killer patrol the edge of the car lot, their heads down as they sniff the ground. The shed has a rickety door and smells like mold—and worse. I peek inside through a crack in the doorframe. There's no floor—just rubble with piles of old newspapers scattered on top. This must be where the dogs live when they're not in their crates.

"Don't forget to change their water," Vince says. He's come to check on me. "It's with the kibble in the van."

The dogs' water goes in a dented tin bowl. I rinse the bowl as best I can before I refill it.

"You look like you're doing okay, kid," Vince tells me.

Soon, I think, I'll tell him my name is Justin—not kid. Maybe when he pays me at the end of my shift.

But when the end of my shift finally comes, I don't get paid. My lower back aches from dragging around crates and scooping poop. There was even more of it at the next two stops—another car lot and a construction site.

"Whatcha waiting for?" Floyd says when they drop me off near our apartment.

"Uh," I say, stumbling for words, "I, uh, thought I'd get paid at the end of my shift. Vince said—"

"Vince said nothing," Floyd says. "I'm the boss. You get paid Fridays."

So there won't be any T-bone steak for us—or for Smokey. Not tonight anyway.

"See ya tomorrow, kid. Same time," Vince says when I jump out of the van. I figure that means they're keeping me.

chapter five

"Why are you home so late?" Dad's back is to me. It's not dark yet, and I can just make out how one rectangular spot is paler than the rest of the wall. There used to be a picture hanging there of Mom and us, but Dad smashed it during a cloudy mood. He broke the frame and shattered the glass, but I fished the picture out of the garbage. Now it's in my bottom drawer, hidden under my socks. I look at it sometimes when Dad isn't around.

I'm glad I kept the picture. After Mom left, I'd sometimes think some lady at the store or on the street was her, but that doesn't happen anymore. To be honest, I'm starting to forget the sound of Mom's voice and what she looked like. The picture helps me remember.

"I...uh, I got a job." I should have told Dad before, but I didn't know how. And with Dad, you never know what'll set off a cloudy mood.

"You got a job? What kind of job would they give a kid like you?" I wonder if Dad's jealous. He's been out of work since July. He used to work for a contractor, doing odd jobs, but they let him go. Dad says it was because the economy tanked. After that, the man who owns our building hired Dad to do some painting, but that didn't work out either. Dad said the job was beneath him.

"It's a job working with dogs. I met this guy Vince at the convenience store, and he said I had a way with dogs and—" I'm talking too quickly. That happens when I get nervous.

"How much are they paying you?"

"Twenty dollars a shift. If I work hard, they'll give me five shifts a week, and sometimes an extra morning shift before school, so that'd come to—"

Dad spins his chair around. He actually looks kind of impressed. "So where's your twenty dollars?"

"I don't get paid till Friday. But Friday's only four more—"

"Friday?" I hate when Dad shouts. Mrs. MacAlear hates it too, which says something considering she's hard of hearing. When Dad shouts, she whacks her broom against the wall between our apartments. "How do you know you'll even see this guy again? How do you know he didn't just rip you off?"

"I don't."

Dad sucks in his bottom lip. "That's right, you don't. Let me tell you something, Justin, you can't trust anybody."

There are two beer bottles on the floor next to Dad's chair. He's worse when he starts drinking before supper. "How about

I make us something to eat?" I say. There's nothing on the hotplate, which means Dad hasn't started supper. And I'm starving.

What if Dad is right—and Vince and Floyd don't end up paying me? No, I can't let myself think like that. They're okay guys. Well, Vince is anyhow. They wouldn't stiff me for the money. They wouldn't take advantage of a kid. Or would they?

"When are we ever going to have something besides mac and cheese?" It sounds like Dad is talking to himself. I decide it's best not to say anything. Maybe he'll calm down.

I pull off my sweatshirt. It's damp from sweat. Then I head for our little kitchen and take a pot out from under the sink. I need to boil the water—or it'll be nine o'clock before we eat.

"I'm talking to you!" Dad says. He heads over to where I am. He's holding an unopened beer bottle.

I look around the apartment. It feels smaller than ever. I think about the dog shed in the used-car lot. Right now, even that shed seems like a better place than where I am.

Dad is so close I can smell the beer on his breath. I take a step back.

"What are you—afraid of me?" Dad is losing it now. "You know I'd never lay a hand on you." His words come out like a sob. An angry sob.

That's true. Dad has never laid a hand on me. But he's done stuff that's almost as bad.

Then, just like that, Dad hurls the beer bottle against the wall. My whole body tenses. The bottle doesn't shatter, but the cap flies off. Beer gushes everywhere, down the wall and onto the floor, making a sticky brown trail. The bottle has left an ugly gash in the plaster.

Next door, Mrs. MacAlear whacks the wall with her broom.

Dad ignores Mrs. MacAlear's whacking. He looks at me. "Are you just going to stand there like a dummy? Or are you going to clean that mess up?"

chapter six

Amanda kicks me under the desk. "Uh, what?" I mumble, straightening up. I know from the sour taste in my mouth I must have dozed off.

"In order to calculate fifteen percent of four hundred and twenty, we need to begin by dividing four hundred and twenty by what number, Justin?" Mrs. Thompson is asking me.

I'm not bad in math, but I'm too tired to think. I've worked after school every day this week, plus an extra shift on Tuesday morning. Then there are all my house chores. My lower back is so sore that when my pencil falls to the floor, I ache too much to pick it up.

Amanda scribbles the number one hundred on the top corner of her notebook— and underlines it twice. "One hundred," I say brightly.

"That's right," Mrs. Thompson says. "And then we need to multiply by what number, Carleen?"

"Thanks," I tell Amanda, mouthing the word. When she hands me my pencil, I give her a grateful nod.

Mrs. Thompson hands out a sheet of problems and explains how she wants us to work in pairs. How do I ask Amanda if she wants to be my partner?

What Mrs. Thompson says next makes me so happy I could kiss her powdery white face. "I want you to pair up by rows. Those of you sitting by the wall will have to—"

I'm not listening anymore. I'm moving my desk so it touches Amanda's.

Amanda turns to make sure Mrs.
Thompson isn't hovering nearby. Then she
draws some crisscross lines on the blank
side of Mrs. Thompson's handout. "How
'bout a quick game of tic-tac-toe?"

"No way," I tell her. "We're supposed to
be doing math."

Amanda turns the handout over, but
I can tell she is not quite ready to get to
work. "How come you're so tired lately?"
she asks.

"I got this part-time job, working with
dogs."

"Cool. I love dogs. We have two
schnauzers. Isabelle and Isidor. They're
the cutest things ever. So do you work at
the mall—in the pet shop?"

"Nope."

"Dog walking?" she asks.

"Nope."

"Well what then?"

I know we should be doing math, but
I also want Amanda to know about the
kind of work I do. "I got a job working
with guard dogs."

Amanda raises her eyebrows. They're the same color red as her hair. "Guard dogs? Aren't they vicious?"

"No way. They're pussycats," I say. Then I think about Killer. "Well, mostly."

"But they're trained to attack, right? So they have to be vicious..."

"They're not. It's more like they're... well...jumpy, you know, nervous. Nervous dogs make the best—"

"Justin, Amanda." Mrs. Thompson frowns at us from under her glasses. "You are working on your percentages, aren't you?"

"Sure we are," Amanda answers for us.

"We've got one more stop," Floyd says once all the dogs have been dropped off at work sites. I don't dare complain. It's Friday, and I've been picturing the steaks— T-bones—I'm going to buy. That is if I get paid today, if Dad's wrong about Floyd and Vince taking advantage of me because I'm a kid.

The motion of the car is making me dozy. My eyelids feel heavy. I'm trying to stay awake, but it's hard. I feel Floyd watching me in the rearview mirror. "Kid's sleeping on the job," I hear him tell Vince.

"Let him sleep," Vince says. "He's not used to all that shoveling."

I'm only half listening to their conversation now. "I got a call that our friend has some new stock," Floyd tells Vince in a low voice.

"You got the cash for him?" Vince whispers back.

Floyd pats the pocket of his jeans. I'm awake enough to hope my money is there too.

"Terence has himself some sweet deal," I hear Vince say as we cross a bridge that takes us off the island of Montreal. "He gets paid by the city, and then we pay him again."

Floyd brings the van to a stop. We're parked behind a donut shop. "Nap time's over," Floyd announces.

I try not to yawn as I follow Floyd and Vince out of the van. I don't want them to think I don't have the stamina for this job.

A small man with a round red face is waiting for us. He must be Terence. He is standing next to a small truck that says *Animal Control* on it. The truck has a cap on the back. The dogs must be in there.

"Who's that?" he asks when he sees me.

Floyd shrugs. "Just some kid we hired to scoop poop."

"You sure he won't talk?" Terence asks.

"He's not the talking type," Vince says.

Terence nods, but I can tell he's still not sure about me. He looks over his shoulder to make sure no one else is around. "I've got four dogs. All big and mean-lookin'."

I'm starting to understand that guard dogs only need to look mean. It's different from actually being mean.

Floyd and Vince peer into the back of Terence's truck. "They look mean all right," Floyd says, reaching into his pocket for the cash. Now I can see the dogs too. One is a scrawny-looking brown mutt. Terence was right. He looks mean.

"Okay, kid," Floyd says, "show Terence here why we hired you. Get these dogs out of their crates and into ours. You should see this kid scoop poop, Terence. It's his specialty," Floyd adds with a laugh.

"Hey, boy," I tell the brown mutt as I unlatch his crate. He growls. I back away.

Floyd slaps my shoulder. "What are you—scared?"

"I'm not scared." Only I am. Something tells me this dog has never had a rabies shot.

"Lemme give you a hand," Vince says. Together we transfer the mutt into one of our crates. The dog settles down. Maybe he's so tired even a strange crate looks good right now.

The next dog is a German shepherd. Well fed, well groomed—what Smokey might look like if he'd had a different kind of life. This dog's eyes look confused. As if he wants to ask, what in the world is going on?

The next two could be brothers. They're mutts, but I can tell from their rust markings they have rottweiler blood.

I notice the collar when I'm sliding the last crate back into Terence's truck. A brand new green leather collar with silver stars. There's an ID tag on it. I reach for the collar. It must belong to the German shepherd.

Floyd grabs my arm. "What do you think you're doing?" His voice is even sharper than usual. "Leave that right there."

"Junkyard dogs don't need collars," Terence says.

I let the collar fall from my hands. It lands without a sound on the carpeted floor of the truck. "I thought..."

"You don't think nothing," Floyd tells me. "You were hired to scoop poop. Not to think."

Though the letters on the ID tag are upside down, I can see the name *Star* engraved on it. There's a phone number too, but I can't make it out.

One thing I know for sure is Star is not some stray. He's someone's pet. And somehow Terence got hold of him.

"You sure this kid's okay?" Terence asks.

"He's fine," Floyd says, slapping my shoulder again. "Which reminds me, it's payday, ain't it, kid?" He pulls six crisp twenties from his front pocket.

I can practically taste that T-bone steak.

"So, you enjoying this line of work?" Floyd asks as he hands me the bills. I feel his eyes on my face.

The door to the back of our van is open. I hear a dog whimpering. Probably Star. I take the money and swallow hard. "Yes, sir," I tell Floyd. "I sure am."

chapter seven

Even my head is sweaty from shoveling. Now that I'm back in our building, I can take off my cap.

"Why hello, Justin." Mrs. MacAlear pops out from behind the mailboxes.

"How are you, Mrs. MacAlear?" I ask, slipping my cap back on.

"Never mind me," she says. "I'm an old woman. Young people like yourself are far more interesting. Your hair seems to be growing in."

I feel my cheeks get hot. But Mrs. MacAlear is right about my hair. There's fuzzy hair filling in the bare patches. Maybe it's because I'm eating better—or because I'm less worried about how Dad and I are going to pay the bills.

"Have you seen our friend at the convenience store?"

It takes me a minute to realize Mrs. MacAlear means Smokey. "I didn't make it over there today. I had to work."

"Which reminds me," Mrs. MacAlear says, tapping the side of her head, "I have some things for you. Why don't you come along and I'll give them to you straightaway?"

I have never seen the inside of Mrs. MacAlear's apartment. From her doorway, I can see the apartment is packed with knickknacks—crystal vases and porcelain dolls are displayed on shelves, tables and even on the windowsills.

Mrs. MacAlear catches me checking the place out. "Would you like to come in?"

"Uh, maybe another time. My dad's waiting for me."

Mrs. MacAlear disappears into her kitchen. She comes back with two shopping bags filled with empty bottles. "I thought you might want these."

"Thanks a lot," I tell her. "But are you sure you don't want to cash them in yourself?"

Mrs. MacAlear shoos me away. "You'd be doing me a favor if you took them," she says. "Besides, this will give you an excuse to visit your friend."

I'm nearly at the door to our apartment when Mrs. MacAlear calls me back. "I nearly forgot. I have this for you too."

I leave the two bags on the floor. Mrs. MacAlear hands me a hardcover book. It smells old, and there's a cocker spaniel on the cover.

"It's a history of dogs. When I spotted it at the secondhand bookshop, I thought you might enjoy it."

"Are you sure?" It's not like it's my birthday or anything.

"Of course I'm sure." She reaches toward me. The veins on the outside of her hand are thick and blue. Without meaning to,

I take a step back. When Mrs. MacAlear smiles, her eyes close for a second. Even her eyelids are wrinkled. "Let me know whether you like the book."

"Where did that book come from?" Dad asks when I'm settled under the blanket reading.

"The woman next door gave it to me," I say.

"The witch with the broom?" he asks.

"She's not a witch," I say.

"We don't need anyone's charity."

"It's not charity. It's a book about dogs," I say.

Dad groans. He's not done arguing. "Shouldn't you be doing your homework— and not reading some book about dogs?"

"I finished all my homework."

Dad adjusts the pillow on his side of the pullout couch. "So what does the book have to say anyhow?"

I turn to look at Dad, half expecting him to be rolling his eyes, but he isn't.

"Well," I tell him, "it says here the Latin name for dogs is *Canis lupus famil*—" It's not easy to speak Latin.

"*Familiaris*," Dad says. "It means common. *Lupus* means wolf."

"You know Latin?"

"I know a lot of stuff, Latin included."

"It says dogs are a subspecies of the gray wolf. And that dogs are believed to be the first species domesticated by humans."

Dad snorts. "That doesn't say much for dogs, does it? Now cats, they're far more intelligent. No self-respecting cat would fetch a ball or chase a Frisbee."

The thought of a cat chasing a Frisbee makes me laugh. "Maybe getting along with humans is smart," I say.

Dad turns over so he's facing away from me. "Never worked for me," he mutters.

Soon Dad is snoring. I'm tired, but I keep reading. The book says dogs have been around for 15,000 years. That's more than 1,000 times longer than I've been around! There's a section about how dogs were domesticated. There's something called the "garbage theory" that says wolves used to raid ancient peoples' garbage dumps. The wolves that were least afraid of humans got the most food. I think there *is* something smart about getting along with people. I'd way rather be a dog curled up on someone's living room rug than a gray wolf scavenging for food on a freezing day.

I decide to peek at the section on working dogs. *Dogs can learn to perform simple tasks*, the book says. I stop at a picture of a dog pulling a sled over the snow. The book says sled dogs can pull hundreds of pounds.

The dog on the next page is a German shepherd like Smokey that works as a seeing-eye dog. *It's important*, the book says, *that people do not disturb seeing-eye dogs while they work. Seeing-eye dogs need to focus on their task*. I guess it's the same for Smokey. The book also mentions how many dogs seem to enjoy having jobs.

I'm trying to decide whether I like working—or whether I just like making money. I definitely don't like shoveling poop, but I like hanging out with dogs.

I put the book down and pull the blanket up so it nearly covers my chin. As I doze off, I think about working dogs. Maybe there's nothing wrong with making dogs work. Maybe it really is what the book calls "a mutually beneficial arrangement." It's good for the people who need the dogs' help, and good for the dogs too.

I think about those first gray wolves who weren't scared of humans 15,000 years ago. It's like they made a sort of pact—be good to us, and we'll be good to you. We'll help herd your sheep and guard your convenience stores, and in return you feed us and pet us and treat us right.

But then I remember the matted clumps on Smokey's coat, and the way the dogcatcher tried to get rid of that dog collar from the back of his truck...

If those gray wolves had known about Floyd and Terence the dogcatcher, maybe they'd never have come close in the first place.

chapter eight

I don't hear the phone because I'm scrubbing the bathtub. "Turn that darn water off!" Dad bellows from the hallway. "You didn't hear the phone, and then you didn't hear me call you. You know I don't like getting up for nothing. There's a guy on the phone, says he's your boss."

I turn off the faucet. My heart is thumping in my chest. This is the first time Floyd has phoned for me. Something must be wrong.

"Hey, kid, how ya doin'?" Something is definitely wrong if he's asking how I'm doing.

"Look, I know it's Sunday, but I need some help—with a special project. There's fifty bucks in it for you."

"What time do you want to pick me up?" I ask.

When I tell Dad I'll be out, he says, "At least he's paying you for your trouble. Better than that old biddy next door who sends you out to pick up her prescriptions and gives you nothing for it."

The special mission turns out to be a visit to the SPCA. "You go in," Floyd tells me. "Ask to see the dogs. I need a bitch—" He must notice me bristle. "Relax, kid," he says, laughing, "I'm not being rude. I need a bitch—a female dog. Unspayed. That part's important. It'll say so on the card outside the cage. Most of the bitches in there are spayed, so you'll have to look around. And be discreet about it, will ya?"

"Are you going to breed her?"

The scar on Floyd's forehead throbs.

"I know, I know. No questions," I tell him as I hop out of the van.

"Hey, kid," Floyd says, "what's your name anyhow?"

"Justin."

"Well, Justin, I need some gas. I'll meet you inside in"—Floyd checks his watch—"fifteen minutes. And one more thing, what's your old man's name?"

"Ted Leduc." I know better than to ask Floyd why he needs my dad's name. Or to say I know Floyd has a full tank of gas.

A case of air freshener couldn't mask the smell of dog at the SPCA. A cheerful woman with curly blond hair leads me to the dogs that are up for adoption. She tells me her name is Glenda and that she volunteers here on Sundays. "You're welcome to have a look. But because you're under eighteen, you'll have to have an adult come back with you if you're serious about adopting."

Glenda doesn't have to tell me we're nearing the dog room. I hear the barking and howling from down the hall. The smell of poop and pee is even stronger now.

When I push open the door, I see both sides of the room are lined with cages.

It feels like a prison. Or even worse. It feels like death row.

Some of the dogs press their muzzles against the bars. Some are whimpering. Others huddle at the back of their cages, too afraid to meet me.

I walk down the center aisle. I'm supposed to be looking for an unspayed female, but I want to see the dogs first. One boxer is so old his muzzle is all gray. A couple of dogs are so thin their bones nearly poke through their skin. They must be from one of those puppy mills I read about in the paper. Places where they breed dogs but don't look after them properly.

Glenda shakes her head. "We're full up, what with the last puppy mill. We've got hardly any room for new arrivals. Things are almost as bad here as they were back in July on moving day."

I remember back to July 1, moving day in Montreal. There were moving trucks everywhere, holding up traffic. And now that I think about it, I remember how the janitor in the building across the street from ours told me and Dad how a tenant packed all his stuff but left his tabby cat behind.

"You wouldn't believe the number of people who abandon their dogs and cats when they move." Glenda shakes her head as if to say she's seen it all.

I can feel my throat tightening. I'm thinking about all those animals and also about how my mom left me and my dad behind.

I'm glad Glenda can't tell I'm upset. "Are you looking for any kind of dog in particular?" she asks. "Most people want a pup, but training a pup takes a lot of work. I always say, 'Go for an older dog instead.' Your mom and dad okay with adopting a dog?"

"They're coming 'round to it," I say, and immediately I feel bad about lying.

I decide not to ask about unspayed females. The last thing I need is for Glenda to think that I've come for a breeding dog for a puppy mill.

There's a chocolate-Lab mix in the next cage. "That girl's still kind of young. Hasn't been spayed," Glenda tells me.

The door to the dog room opens. "Hi, Son," Floyd says. "Fall in love with a dog, yet?"

He turns to Glenda. "Justin's birthday's coming up, and he wants a dog. I told him we'd be doing a good thing if we adopted one."

Floyd's loving-father routine catches me off guard. When Glenda turns her head, he gives me a stern look.

"Justin likes this girl over here," Glenda says, gesturing for Floyd to follow her.

Floyd reads the card taped onto the outside of the cage. "So she hasn't been spayed?" You can't tell from his voice whether he thinks that's a good thing. Floyd is a way better actor than I would have guessed.

"We do recommend that all the dogs that leave here are spayed or neutered. We have a vet on the premises who'll do the operation at a disc—"

"No problem," Floyd cuts Glenda off. "We've got a friend who's a vet, and we'd like to give him the business, wouldn't we, Justin?"

Floyd peers into the cage. "Aren't you a lovely girl?"

There is paperwork to do. "Your name, please," Glenda says to Floyd.

Floyd shoots me a look before he answers. "Ted Leduc."

I suck in my breath. Why didn't Floyd tell her his real name?

When Glenda asks for ID, Floyd makes a fuss. "Can you believe it?" He whacks the side of his head with a brochure. "I was so excited about getting Justin a dog, I forgot my license at home."

"Do you have your Medicare card?" Glenda asks.

"It's with my license. Justin, show Glenda here your school ID. That'll do, won't it, Glenda? Kid's my son after all." Floyd throws his arm around my shoulder. Floyd is scary when he tries acting nice.

Glenda takes my ID card. "I just need to go to the office to make a photocopy of this. I'll only be a minute," she says.

Floyd waits until she has closed the door behind her. "There's one more thing," he whispers. He's using his rough voice again. "Don't mention this to Vince. He thinks I already have too many pets. This'll be our little secret, okay?"

I can feel him waiting for an answer.

"Okay," I tell him.

When Glenda gets back, she hands me my ID. Another volunteer brings the dog. The dog licks the outside of my hand.

Floyd pets her head. "Ain't you a beauty?" Then he turns to me. "Happy birthday, Son."

Glenda flashes us a big smile. "Nothing makes me feel better," she says, "than when our animals go to good people."

That makes Floyd laugh. "We're good people all right, ain't we?" Floyd gives me a nudge.

To be honest, I'm not so sure.

chapter nine

When the van pulls up on Friday afternoon and Vince isn't in the passenger seat, the muscles in my stomach tighten. I don't like the idea of being alone with Floyd again. I'm more nervous around him than I am around the guard dogs. But it's payday, so I climb into the front seat.

"Hey, kid," a raspy voice says, and I relax. Vince is driving. "Floyd's under the weather. It's just us today."

"My name's Justin," I say in a quiet voice.

At first I think Vince doesn't hear me. The radio is on, and he is humming along to some country-and-western song. "Well, Justin, I want to say I think you've been doing a fine job. And I'm taking the credit"—Vince takes one hand off the wheel to thump his chest—"for finding you."

"Th—thanks." I can hardly get the word out I'm smiling so hard.

Vince helps me lug the crates to the back of the van. He's nicer when Floyd's not around. "Uh-oh," Vince says when he unlatches King's crate.

There's a jagged gash caked with dry blood on the side of King's neck. King growls when Vince runs his finger along the gash. "Something must've happened to him in the lot last night. Maybe he got caught on the fence. The technician who picked him up this morning should've spotted it."

"Should we get him to a vet?"

Vince shakes his head. "We don't bother much with vets. Vet visits cut into Floyd's profits. Nah, I should be able to stitch him up."

We have to force King's snout into a muzzle. Then I hold his head while Vince washes the wound with antiseptic.

Vince bites his lower lip as he works. When he presses down on the gash, King's spine stiffens. "It's gonna be okay, boy," Vince tells him. "But I don't think you're gonna be doing much guard work tonight. We'd better let you nap in that fancy condo of yours."

"Get me the emergency case from the glove compartment, will ya?" Vince says when he's done cleaning the wound.

I wince when Vince takes out a sewing needle and a spool of surgical thread. The thread looks like dental floss. "Don't worry, kid. Dog's gonna be just fine. Keep a hold of him, okay? Look away if you want to."

In the end, I don't look away. I watch as the needle pierces King's fur, then goes out and back in again. King's eyes are glassy. His tail droops between his legs, and his whole body shakes as Vince stitches him up. I put my arms around King to steady him. I feel as if somehow, if I'm strong enough, I can take away King's pain.

The needle weaves in and out again. Vince never lifts his eyes from the tip of the needle. It takes eight stitches to close the gash. King is panting now. "It's all done, boy," I tell him.

"Pass me that tube of antibiotic cream." Vince applies cream over the stitches. "Keep a hold of him so he doesn't try to rub it off," Vince tells me.

King leans his body into mine. He tries to scratch the wound with his hind leg, but I don't let him. "How'd you get a gash like that anyhow?" I ask him. When King looks up, I get the feeling he wishes he could tell me.

"I'll shovel today," Vince says, reaching into the back of the van for the shovel.

"You sure?"

"I'm sure. You seen enough poop these last couple of weeks to last you a lifetime. Besides, you're doing good looking after that dog. I'll say one thing—you sure got a way with animals."

Later, I help Vince take King into the condo. We get him settled on a bed of newspapers. "It ain't the Ritz, but it'll have to do ya," Vince tells the dog. "It's a good thing Floyd's got the flu, or he'd have put you to work. Listen," Vince says, turning to me, "what Floyd don't know can't hurt him. So let's not tell him King spent a night in here. The other dogs can do the rounds, and nobody'll be the wiser."

"Makes sense to me," I say.

On the drive back, Vince turns up the music. At first, I don't even realize I'm singing along to the music too.

Vince looks over at me and laughs.

"How do they debark dogs?" I ask when we've been driving for a while.

"Sure you want to know?"

I hesitate for a moment. "Yup, I'm sure."

"The vet'll do it, but it's costly. There's people who'll shove a pipe down a puppy's throat."

I feel my own throat tighten. How could anyone be so cruel? "Did you ever do it?" I ask.

Vince turns to look at me. "Nope, not me. But I've seen it done. It's not pretty. But you get to be my age, Justin, and you learn to live with things. 'Specially if you need your paycheck the way me and my old lady do."

The music is still on, but neither of us sings along. Vince doesn't say anything more until we're exiting the highway. "Listen, kid, er, Justin, you're gonna have to wait till Monday for your cash. Floyd's in charge of finances."

Vince must see from my face that I'm disappointed. "Hey now," he says, "don't worry about it." Then he reaches into his front pocket and takes out a fifty-dollar bill. "How 'bout I give you half from my own money, and we straighten things out with Floyd on Monday?"

"That'd be great. I've got some shopping to do."

"What are you into—computer games or CDs or something like that?" he asks.

"Yeah, something like that," I say.

Vince drops me off outside our building. Floyd usually makes me walk from the corner. Vince puts his hand on my forearm. I can tell he has something else to tell me.

"What is it?"

Vince bites his lower lip, the way he did when he was stitching King. Then he turns off the motor. "I'm afraid I've got some bad news," he says. "That German shepherd at the convenience store is getting too old to work. Floyd says we're gonna have to get rid of him."

"Get rid of him?" I don't mean to shout.

"Business is business," Vince tells me. "What Floyd says goes. If a dog gets too old to work, he's no good to us anymore." He claps me on the shoulder. "Like I said before, sometimes you gotta learn to live with things."

chapter ten

My body goes cold when I don't see Smokey behind the counter. I have to do something, so I buy the Saturday paper. I left home in such a hurry, I forgot my empties.

"Where's the dog?" I ask the cashier. It says Edward on his shirt. I try to make it sound like I'm just asking.

Edward rings up the newspaper. "That'll be a buck fifty. Dog's out for a walk. Have a good day." My body begins to relax. Smokey's not gone—at least not yet.

Outside, I peer up and down Monkland Avenue. At first, I don't see Smokey, but then I spot him. He's with Pete.

Smokey is sniffing a corner of a dumpster, but he looks up when I approach. His eyes are clear and bright. Vince must be wrong about Smokey.

But when Smokey walks, I notice one of his rear legs dragging. I read in Mrs. MacAlear's book that German shepherds are prone to a condition called hip dysplasia. Is that what's wrong with Smokey?

"How ya doin'?" I ask Pete.

"I'm good. Kind of excited actually." This is the most Pete has said to me in all the time I've been coming to the convenience store.

"What're you excited about?" I ask.

"I thought you knew. This is Smokey's last week on the job. We're getting a new dog on Monday, another shepherd. No offense to you"—he looks at Smokey—"but we need a newer model."

"What's gonna happen to Smokey?" I ask.

"Why're you asking me? You're the one in the guard-dog business."

There's an extra crate in the van on Monday afternoon, and I know without asking that Smokey's inside.

All shift, I feel nauseous. Shoveling makes the feeling worse.

"What's with you today, kid?" Floyd asks. Floyd hasn't bothered to use my name since our visit to the SPCA.

"What are we gonna do with the shepherd in the crate?" I ask him.

Floyd punches my shoulder a little too hard. "You forget what I told you about asking questions?"

"I've got a cramp in my leg," I tell Floyd. "Mind if I sit in the back of the van?"

"Suit yourself," he says.

All the dogs have been delivered to their work sites. It's just me and Smokey in the back now. "Hi, Smokester," I whisper, slipping my hand between the bars so I can stroke the top of his head.

Smokey rests his head on the bottom of the cage. He wants me to keep petting him. I wonder how long it's been since someone petted him. I wonder, too, how Smokey got debarked. Did a vet do it, or did someone else, maybe Floyd, do it? I blink to make the picture in my mind disappear, but it won't.

And where are we taking Smokey now? The SPCA? It's not a bad place, but they've got more abandoned dogs than they can handle. They'll put Smokey up for adoption, but who knows if anyone will take him. Most people want puppies—not aging German shepherds who walk funny.

From what I can tell, we're not going to the SPCA. We're headed out of town—in the same direction we went to meet Terence. Will Terence take Smokey? I can't decide if that would be better or worse than leaving him at the SPCA.

If only I could adopt Smokey. But that would never work. Our building has a no-pets rule. Besides, Dad would never agree to it. It costs money to look after a dog, and even now that I'm working, Dad and

I barely have enough to look after ourselves.

We're off the island, and there are fewer streetlamps. "Are you sure there's nothing else we can do?" Vince asks Floyd.

"You getting soft or what?" Floyd says to the front window.

Smokey's ears prick up as if he is eavesdropping too.

"Okay, then, you're the boss. You call the shots," Vince says.

"Exactly," says Floyd.

I keep my eyes on the road signs. We pass Île Perrot.

"What if Terence picks him up?"

Floyd laughs. "Wouldn't that be somethin'?"

As the van slows down, Smokey looks up at me. "Don't worry," I tell him.

"Whatcha doin' back there? Chatting up the dog? Think you're the dog whisperer or what?" Floyd says.

"He knows the dog from the convenience store." Vince sounds tired.

"That dog's too old to be any use to anyone. They'll euthanize him at the SPCA,"

Floyd says. "So we're gonna give him a chance to make it on his own."

"Here?" I say. We're at the side of the road in the middle of nowhere. Floyd can't be serious. What is Smokey going to do out here?

"I thought I already talked to you about asking questions. You let the dog out. This is as good a place as any. And make it quick, will ya?"

I hear what Floyd is saying, but it's not making any sense. He taps the steering wheel. "C'mon," he says, "let the dog out. Now!"

Letting Killer out of his cage that first time was nothing compared to this. My fingers tremble as I fumble with the latch. I'll never forget the look in Smokey's eyes. It says, *I trust you.*

If I do this, I'm no better than the people who abandon their pets on moving day. Do those dogs give their owners the same trusting look Smokey is giving me?

Another car flies by so quickly I can't tell what color it is. There's a small forest to the right, but if Smokey runs out onto the road, he'll be dead for sure. That's when I realize this is all part of Floyd's plan. It's less trouble than taking Smokey to the SPCA— and cheaper than having him euthanized by the vet. My head is spinning.

Honk! Floyd is getting impatient. The honking startles me, but not Smokey. He's still looking at me.

Honk!

It's hard to think straight.

"Stay," I tell Smokey. It's a command he's used to, but how long can I expect Smokey to stay in one place, especially out in the dark like this?

Floyd opens the driver's-side door. "Will ya get back in the van?" he shouts. Then he slams the door shut.

Once I'm back inside the van, I crouch next to Smokey's empty cage. It still smells like him.

I don't look out the back window. If I did, I wouldn't be able to see anything anyhow—on account of the tears.

chapter eleven

Vince pats my elbow when I get out of the van. I wonder if he can tell I've been crying. "You gotta be tough to make it in this world," he says. I can see from his eyes he feels bad too. But he needs Floyd's money as much as I do. Maybe that's why he won't stand up to him.

"See ya tomorrow," I manage to say.

As I trudge downstairs to our apartment, I think maybe I'm not tough enough to make it in this world.

I hear a creaking noise. Mrs. MacAlear pokes her head out from behind her door and gestures for me to come over. "Everything all right with you, dear?" she asks. I'm starting to wonder if she waits for me to get home every day after work.

I shake my head. "It's Smokey."

"You shouldn't be smoking," Mrs. MacAlear says, wagging her finger. "It's a terrible habit. Very hard to quit."

If I weren't so broken up, I might laugh. "I don't smoke. It's Smokey."

"Oh," she says, "is that what you call the dog from the convenience store?"

"He's not at the store anymore," I say. "He's in trouble."

"Well then, young man," Mrs. MacAlear says, "you're going to have to do something about that." This time when she reaches toward me, I don't step away. She lays a wrinkly hand on the middle of my back. The way she touches me makes me straighten my shoulders.

"Don't you have to learn to live with things?" I ask.

Mrs. MacAlear leaves her hand on my back. I can tell she is thinking. When she speaks her voice sounds surprisingly young for an old lady. "Not when it comes to the things you can't live with."

"What'll I tell my dad?"

"I'll deal with him." Then she gives me a nudge toward the staircase. "You go deal with Smokey."

Maybe I'm not used to good things happening. Because when I get onto the bus that goes off-island, and I see Amanda smiling at me from across the aisle, I can't believe it's her. I notice how her nose and cheeks are sprinkled with tiny freckles. She has one of those little suitcases on wheels with her.

"Why are you looking at me like that?" she asks me.

"I didn't expect to see you here. What are you doing—running away from home?"

Amanda laughs. "Why would I do that? I'm going to sleep over at my nana's. Her house is right by the bus stop, so I'll be there before dark. My parents don't like me out in the dark alone."

Out in the dark alone. I check my watch. I let Smokey out of the van thirty-four minutes ago.

"Where are you going?" Amanda asks.

"I've gotta take care of some work stuff," I say.

The brakes squeal as the bus stops in front of a coffee shop. A guy with a gray ponytail gets on. "How much?" he asks the driver.

Hurry up, I think. Once the guy has fished the right change from his pocket, the driver puts on the emergency signal lights. They sound like a clock ticking. The driver stands up and stretches. I will him to get back into his seat and drive so I can get to Smokey. Instead the driver steps off the bus.

"I thought you worked on a van," Amanda says. "The one that picks you up after school."

"This is different. Something bad happened to one of our dogs...to Smokey."

Amanda's green eyes widen. "What happened?"

I don't want to tell her. I'm upset enough already.

"C'mon, tell me," she says.

I'm tapping my foot against the floor.

"And quit tapping—you're making me nervous," she says.

The driver gets back on the bus. He's carrying a cup of coffee. Thank goodness the light is green.

"The boss thinks Smokey is getting too old to work...and so, so..." This part is hard to tell. "We left him by the side of the highway." Saying the words out loud makes me feel even worse.

"You what?" Amanda asks.

"Don't shout." I get the feeling the other passengers might be listening to our conversation.

"You left a dog by the side of the highway, and you expect me not to shout? How could you do something like that?"

I don't want Amanda to see me cry. I try taking a deep breath. "That's why I'm going back—to find Smokey."

Amanda is quiet for a moment. She is

either thinking, or she's getting ready to yell again. But then she takes her cell phone out of her backpack. "I'm calling Nana to tell her I'll be late," she says. "I'm going with you, Justin."

"I think this is the stop," I tell Amanda when we pass the sign for Île Perrot.

"You *think* this is it?" she says. I'm afraid she's going to start shouting again.

"I was sitting in the back of the van. With the dog. I couldn't see too well."

"Who let him out?"

I was hoping Amanda wouldn't ask that. I look down at my sneakers. "I did."

When we get off the bus, we see red lights flashing on the road in front of us. Is it a police car? Are we too late? Has Smokey been hit?

Without planning to, I grab Amanda's hand and squeeze it.

Amanda peers into the darkness and squeezes my hand back. "There's a car pulled over. It's probably just a speeding ticket."

I scan the road up ahead, then turn to look behind me. I don't see any sign of Smokey.

There is a small forest to our right. Is this where we left Smokey? There were definitely trees. It's hard to know for sure. Why didn't I pay more attention when Floyd stopped the van?

Something about the clearing behind me looks familiar. "That way," I say, pointing toward it. "At least I think it's that way."

The wheels on Amanda's suitcase clatter on the asphalt. "Smokey!" she calls into the night air.

"Calling for Smokey won't work," I tell her. "Smokey's not really his name."

Amanda parks her suitcase. "So what name should we call?"

"He doesn't have a name. Most people just call him Dog."

"That's the most pathetic thing I ever heard. Imagine not having a name." Amanda starts dragging her suitcase along the side of the road again. "Dog!" she shouts. "Dog!"

chapter twelve

"So how come you call him Smokey?"

We're walking single file. I've offered to cart Amanda's suitcase, and she's behind me.

"I dunno. He seems like a Smokey. His muzzle is the color of smoke."

"What are we going to do with Smokey once we find him?" she asks.

"If we find him."

"Did anyone ever tell you you're very negative?"

A truck flies by. A cloud of dust rises from the asphalt. "Did anyone ever tell you that you shouldn't walk so close to the traffic?"

Amanda edges closer to where the pavement ends. There's a narrow rubble path between the highway and the forest. Is Smokey out there somewhere?

"Dog! Dog!" Amanda and I call out together.

"Dog! Dog!" Our words echo back at us.

Where could Smokey be?

"I bet Smokey'll bark if he hears us," Amanda says.

I like that she calls him Smokey. "He can't bark," I say quietly. I hope she won't start shouting again. Amanda is a very emotional person.

"He can't bark?" At least she sounds calm.

"A lot of guard dogs get debarked. That way they can sneak up on a burglar—and they don't disturb the neighbors." I don't have the heart to tell her how some dogs get debarked.

Amanda harrumphs. "It's not natural for a dog not to bark. Imagine a cat that couldn't purr. Or a bird that doesn't sing."

We trudge along in silence. I'm listening for any sound that might tell us Smokey is out there, but all I hear are cars whizzing by. I hope Smokey knows to stay away from the highway. I can't imagine what must be going through his dog brain. The convenience store is open twenty-four hours a day, so Smokey's not accustomed to being alone. If it were me, I'd panic. What do dogs do when they panic? Run out into traffic?

"What's with your hair anyhow?" Amanda asks.

No one ever asks about my hair.

Maybe it's because I can't see Amanda's face that answering her question doesn't seem like a big deal. "I've got this thing called alopecia. The nurse thinks it's stress-related. But it's getting better."

"I'm glad." Amanda pauses for a second. I hope she's not going to keep asking about my hair. "I'm sorry you get stressed."

I see something dark up ahead. "D'you think that could be him? Dog!" I call. "Is that you?"

Amanda runs ahead of me. "Dog!"

The shape turns out to be a gnarled old tree trunk. I kick it as we pass it.

"He could be anywhere," I mutter. "I bet he panicked when we took off." I don't like to remember Smokey's eyes.

We hear a car slow down behind us. The car pulls over when it reaches us. A middle-aged woman sticks her head out the passenger window. "What are you two thinking? Do you know how dangerous it is on the highway in the dark like this?"

Her eyes land on Amanda's suitcase. "Are you in some kind of trouble?"

"We're looking for a dog," Amanda tells her. "Have you seen a German shepherd?"

The man driving leans over so we can see him too. "Funny, I thought I noticed something in the woods back there. About an eighth of a mile back, maybe less. Could've been a dog, now that I think about it."

"You didn't say anything to me," the woman tells him.

"It happened too quickly. Besides you were yakking. As usual," he adds.

I tug on Amanda's sleeve. "Let's go. An eighth of a mile isn't far."

"Are you sure you're going to be all right?" the man asks.

"Stay as far away from the road as you can. And if the dog runs onto the highway, don't follow him," the woman says.

It's faster to carry Amanda's suitcase. The two of us sprint down the side of the road. The rubble slows us down, but at least we have a sense we're headed in the right direction.

I pause and raise a finger in the air. Did I just hear something?

"Dog! Dog!" Amanda shouts. Her red hair flaps around her face.

Now she hears it too. A whimper. It's hoarse-sounding, but it's a whimper all right.

"Dog! Smokey!"

Up ahead is a boulder, covered in dark velvety moss. When the boulder moves,

I know it's Smokey, crouched in the dark. I hear him pant as he makes his way between the trees. When he's close enough, he licks my hand. He won't take his eyes off mine.

"See," I tell him, "I came back for you. Smokey, I want you to meet Amanda."

I can't be sure it's not a coincidence, but his tail wags when he hears the name Smokey.

chapter thirteen

"My parents say to tell you they'll take care of Smokey's food," Amanda says when she meets me outside the apartment with a case full of cans. "This stuff is good for senior dogs." We stash the case behind the building.

"Thank your parents for me, okay?"

"They're happy to help. I tried talking them into adopting Smokey. My mom would do it, but Dad says three dogs is too much for one house. And that Mom and

I would have to choose between him and Smokey, which I guess means no."

I know Smokey can't live in the furnace room forever. But for now, it's the only plan I've got. I never knew a dog could sleep so much. Every time I peek inside, Smokey is curled up like a giant furry S. Smokey can't bark, but he sure can snore. He hardly moves from the pile of old blankets by the furnace. And he loves that canned food Amanda brought over. He started wolfing it down before I even finished emptying the can.

I wait until after Dad is asleep to visit Smokey. I've been walking him late at night so no one from the building will see us. I'm really careful about the noise. So far not even Mrs. MacAlear knows he's there. She loves dogs, but something tells me she's a stickler for rules.

"Hey, Smokey," I wave a tug toy in front of me. The girl at the pet store in the mall said it's the most popular toy for a dog his size.

Smokey thumps his tail against the floor when I come closer, but he does not even look at the toy. I wave it some more. Still no reaction. I stick the toy right in front of his muzzle, but he doesn't grab for it the way the girl in the pet store said he would.

I try rubbing the toy against Smokey's muzzle, then pulling it away quickly. There, that should work. But instead of tugging on the rope the way he's supposed to, Smokey lets the toy fall to the ground. He looks up at me like he can't figure out what he's supposed to do.

I crouch down and wave the toy in front of Smokey again. I toss it so it lands at his feet. Still nothing.

That's when I realize what's going on. Smokey doesn't know how to play. He never learned how. He was too busy being a guard dog. No wonder he's so tired now.

I plop down on the ground in front of him and pet him under his chin the way he likes. "Let me show you how this works."

I put the toy near his mouth, and this time Smokey takes it. This time, I don't pull hard on the toy. Smokey pulls back, but just a bit. Now we're getting somewhere. When I pull another time, Smokey's ears prick up for a second, but he forgets to pull back. I let it give, then I tug harder. Smokey pulls back—now he's watching the toy.

"Thatta boy," I tell him as I stroke his coat.

I nearly forgot to air out the furnace room. Yesterday, when I was doing dishes, Dad said I smelled like dog. Dad will have a fit if he learns Smokey is living down the hall. In a way, Smokey's not being able to bark has turned out to be a good thing. But I have to do something about the smell. Leaving the window open should help.

When I get up to open the window, Smokey is examining the toy. He still looks like he's not quite sure what it's doing on his blanket.

It's only when I've pried open the window that I notice something I didn't see before—a box of dog treats on the water heater.

Someone else knows Smokey is here. The door is closed, but I look around the furnace room just the same. There's no one here but me and Smokey.

"Wanna go for your walk?"

Smokey gets up from his bed. His hips seem extra stiff today.

The TV is on in Mrs. MacAlear's apartment. She's probably been looking in on Smokey, giving him treats.

I rush Smokey out of the building, relaxing only when we're halfway down the block. I've been walking him down the alleyways in our neighborhood, where the dog people hang out.

After Smokey has done his business and is settled back in the furnace room, I knock on Mrs. MacAlear's door.

The news is on, so I have to knock several times. I can feel her peering at me through the peephole in her door.

"It's just me, Mrs. MacAlear."

She is wearing a turquoise velvet housecoat and black Chinese slippers. "Is everything all right, Justin?" she asks as she opens the door.

"I...er...just wanted to say thanks."

Mrs. MacAlear looks puzzled. "For the book? You've already thanked me. There's no need to thank me again. I've been meaning to ask you, Justin, how did things go with the dog the other night?"

If Mrs. MacAlear didn't leave the dog treats, then who did?

chapter fourteen

"What the heck's going on?" Vince asks when Floyd turns into the car lot.

I'm still half asleep in the backseat. One of the other technicians has the flu, so I'm doing a morning shift.

"Beats me," Floyd says to the front window.

Two police cruisers block the entrance to the lot. The area around the dog condo is cordoned off with yellow tape.

"Where are the dogs?" I ask. Every other morning I've worked, King and Killer have been patrolling behind the wire fence when we arrive. But there's no sign of them.

A man with slicked-back hair is waving his arms in our direction. It's Mr. Thérrien, the manager of the dealership. Until now, I've only seen him through the windows of the showroom. He signals that he wants to talk to Floyd. Now.

Floyd lowers his window. "G'morning, sir. It looks like there's been trouble," he says in an even voice. "And I don't see my dogs."

"Don't talk to me about your dogs!" Mr. Thérrien snaps. "They're useless! Absolutely useless! Do you have any idea what happened here last night?" His skin is so tanned it looks orange.

"No idea, sir."

"Three cars were stolen! Three! Driven right out of the lot! One was a red convertible—our deluxe model!"

I remember how much Floyd liked that convertible. But when I look at his face, he's not giving anything away.

"And those dogs of yours didn't do a thing to stop it!" Mr. Thérrien is so angry spittle has formed at the corners of his mouth.

Vince leans over from the passenger seat. "Where are my dogs?"

"Your dogs are out back. In a cage!" The manager spits out the words.

"In a cage?" Vince says. "Whose cage?"

The manager's eyes look like they're about to pop out of their sockets. "I guess the robbers brought their own cage. And those stupid dogs of yours walked right into it. To think about the thousands I've been paying you crooks!"

Floyd turns off the motor and steps out of the car. Vince gets out too. Nobody tells me what to do, so I watch from the backseat.

"I don't appreciate you calling us crooks," Floyd tells the manager. "Killer and King are two of our top dogs."

Vince scratches his head.

Several police officers join the manager, Vince and Floyd. One of the police officers is on a cell phone, describing the stolen cars. "A red Miata," he says. "Tan leather interior."

Another officer jots down information in a notebook. "Let's have a look at the dogs," I hear her say. "See if we can figure out what happened here."

There's no way I'm going to miss out on this. When they head for the dog condo, I jump out of the van. "Who're you?" the woman police officer asks when she spots me tagging behind them.

"He's just a kid who helps out on the van," Floyd says. When the officer turns around, Floyd catches my eye. Too quickly for anyone but me to notice, he makes a zipper motion over his lips. I nod to show him I understand.

King and Killer are in a double dog cage. I can tell from the way they are shifting around they don't want to be there. Is it my imagination, or do the dogs look embarrassed—the way kids look when they're waiting outside the principal's office?

"Useless animals!" the manager says again, though he keeps his distance from the cage.

Vince unlatches the cage. Floyd pokes at the dogs and checks their eyes. "Dogs look fine," he says. "They haven't been drugged."

Vince notices a towel. It's faded green with tattered ends. The dogs have been lying on it. When Vince fishes it out of the cage, both dogs start to growl. What is it about that towel?

"Cut it out, will ya?" Vince tells the dogs. He lifts the towel to his face, sniffing it just like a dog would.

"I think I get it," he says. "I'll bet you anything a bitch in heat slept on this towel. No wonder these two boys got distracted."

The woman police officer chews on the end of her pen. "Are you saying the thieves used the towel to deactivate the dogs?"

Vince puts his hands on his hips. "That's exactly what I'm saying, ma'am."

Floyd whistles. "Sounds like some pretty smart crooks." This time, he makes a point of not looking at me.

chapter fifteen

I don't know what to do except quit. The money's great, but I can't keep working, knowing how Floyd treats dogs and suspecting he was involved with the theft at the used-car lot. I can still hear him saying how good he'd look behind the wheel of that red convertible. Why else would he get an unspayed dog? There are too many coincidences, and thinking about them makes me feel sick.

I wait till Dad goes out, and then I phone Vince. "Look," I say, "I need to concentrate on my schoolwork. Since I started working, I haven't been pulling in the grades my folks expect." It's a lie, but saying the word "folks" makes me feel, if only for a moment, that I have a better life.

"I'm sorry to hear that, kid...I mean Justin. You're a good worker. Floyd'll be sorry too. You sure there's nothing we can do to get you to stay? Reduce your hours? Pay you a little more?"

I take a deep breath. Unless I find another job, there'll be no more steaks for Dad and me, and no more leftovers for Smokey. "I'm sure."

I feel better already.

A little later, Dad comes back with the paper. He's muttering to himself when he walks in. "This paper is getting smaller all the time," he says, "and it's not like they're charging any less for it. Soon there'll be no paper at all. What kind of world is that going to be, Justin? Tell me that!" Dad is shouting now. My eyes scan the floor around his feet. Thank goodness there is nothing for him to throw.

I know Dad expects an answer. "Not a very good world," I say in my calmest voice. "D'you feel like a cup of tea, Dad?"

Dad settles down once he has his tea and is reading the newspaper. "It says here there's been a rash of car thefts at auto lots. Not just in Quebec, but Ontario too."

"Let me see." It's hard to read the paper over Dad's back. If he weren't so moody, I'd get closer. "It says the Ontario car lots were patrolled by guard dogs too."

Dad stretches his arms out in front of him. "I wonder if there's some connection between the crimes. What do you think?"

"I wonder too."

"You know, this gives me a bad feeling about the guard-dog business. I appreciate the money you're bringing in, but I was thinking...maybe it's time you quit. Concentrate on school instead."

I nearly flop over onto Dad's chair.

"Look," he says, "just because school didn't work out for me doesn't mean it won't work out for you. You've got a good head on your shoulders and"—here Dad hesitates—"you're good with people. Better than I am."

"But we need the money."

"I thought about that too. I've been looking into doing some tutoring. Just one student at a time. Even someone as difficult as me should be able to manage that." Dad laughs.

It's the first time I've ever heard him admit he was difficult.

I wish I could tell Dad everything—about what it's like working with the dogs, my suspicions about Floyd and how Smokey is living down the hall. But I know he could turn on me at any moment. In the end, I work on my fractions while Dad dozes in his chair. Even when he is asleep, he makes grumbling sounds.

Amanda said she'd meet me if I took Smokey out for a walk at ten. Dad is asleep, and there is no sign of Mrs. MacAlear. Smokey's ears perk up when he sees his leash.

Amanda isn't there, so I figure we'll just walk up and down the street behind the apartment. We head past the tennis club. It's dark except for the streetlights.

I try to calculate how many years till I can get my own place and wonder if Smokey will still be alive then. I sure hope so.

That's when I feel a hand on my shoulder and hear a laugh that sounds like a bark.

"I didn't know you got yourself a dog."

"I—I went back for him." But Floyd knows that. "What are you doing here?"

Floyd rolls his eyes. "You haven't learned, have you? You keep asking questions."

"I quit. You can't tell me what to do anymore." When the words are out of my mouth, I can't quite believe I said them.

"I wanted to talk to you about that, Justin. I want you to keep working on the van."

"I'm through," I say.

But when I look into Floyd's eyes, I feel trapped—like I'll never be able to quit. Smokey growls and tugs on his leash. He wants to get away from Floyd too.

I take a deep breath. "I don't like how you treat dogs."

That makes Floyd laugh. "I treat 'em fine. Besides, they're working dogs. Unless they get old and lame like this sad sack." When Floyd extends the front of his leg, I try pulling Smokey away, but I'm too late. Smokey makes a whimpering noise when Floyd kicks him.

"You gotta keep working for me," Floyd says.

"No, I don't." And then I pull out my best card. The one I've been saving. "I could go to the cops. Tell them about the female dog you got from the SPCA. You used that dog to rob the car lot, didn't you?"

Now, I hope, Floyd will leave me and Smokey alone. But that's not how it goes. "I didn't adopt no dog. Nah, some guy named Ted Leduc adopted that bitch you're talking about. I believe he's your pop. Which means, Sonny Boy," Floyd says, his dark eyes shining, "you'll keep working for me till I say otherwise."

My ears feel hot. I'm not just angry with

Floyd. I'm angry with all the people I never got angry with before—my mom for leaving me, my dad for messing up his life, even Pete at the convenience store for treating me like I was invisible. "I'm done working for you. I'll tell the cops what really happened. And I'll tell them how you treat your dogs."

When Floyd raises his hand, I'm ready for the slap. I don't care if it hurts, if it burns my skin, if it leaves a mark that'll never go away. Because for once in my life, I stood up for myself. And for what's right.

Floyd aims for my cheek, but his hand never touches my skin. Smokey leaps up and hurls himself against Floyd, and Floyd collapses on the ground.

When Smokey bares his yellow teeth, Floyd shields his face with his hand. Smokey may be old, but he can still scare a crook. Floyd isn't going anywhere.

I hear footsteps and then Amanda's voice. "It's okay, Justin," she calls out. "Everything's okay. The police are on their way."

chapter sixteen

Smokey is waiting by the front door of the Iversons' house. In the end, they adopted him, and Mr. Iverson didn't move out.

Smokey's tail is wagging, his ears are pricked up and he is looking out at the street. He may be retired, but he still has guard-dog instincts. "How ya doin', Smokester?" I ask, scratching under his chin.

I smell garlic. "Is your dad coming too?" Mr. Iverson calls from the kitchen.

"Uh-huh," I say. "But he's tutoring till five thirty. Thanks for inviting him tonight too."

"Any friend of Smokey's is a friend of ours," Mrs. Iverson says.

It turned out Dad was the one giving Smokey treats. Once Dad heard the whole story, he even tried talking the landlord into letting us keep Smokey. Mrs. MacAlear said she'd pitch in too. But the landlord wouldn't budge. Somehow, I think it's better this way. The Iversons have a big lawn, and Smokey has Isabelle and Isidor for company. Those little dogs treat him like he's royalty.

Mrs. Iverson hands Amanda and me plates and cutlery so we can set the table. "How's the guard-dog business going?" Mrs. Iverson asks.

"It's going good. Vince and I returned that shepherd I told you about to his family. The kids were so happy they started to cry."

I didn't have to quit my job after all. The police arrested Floyd—he got a reduced sentence because he turned in the mastermind behind the theft ring. Then a guy named James Milne took over the company. Mr. Milne is an animal-rights activist, so he's doing everything he can to improve the way our dogs get treated. Mr. Milne kept Vince and me on.

Dad is a little uncomfortable when he first gets to the Iversons' place. He doesn't know where to sit, and he says "Nice to meet you" twice in a row to Mrs. Iverson. But he relaxes when Smokey comes into the living room and stretches out beside him.

"That's quite a son you've got there," Mr. Iverson tells Dad. "Can you believe he broke up a national car-theft ring?"

Half of me likes the attention. The other half feels embarrassed.

Dad helps me out. "From what I understand, your daughter had something to do it with it too," he tells Mr. Iverson.

The Iversons don't have wine or beer with the spaghetti. I wonder if Amanda told them Dad is trying to cut down on his drinking.

Dad wants to leave after we have the carrot cake Amanda baked for dessert. "If you want to hang out a little longer, we can meet up at the apartment later," he tells me when he gets up from the table.

"How about we play a board game?" Mr. Iverson suggests after we've walked Dad to the door and we're back in the dining room.

"Sure." I'm not used to playing board games.

This reminds me of Smokey and his tug toy. He had to learn how to play. Maybe I can learn too.

"I can't tell you how glad I am that German shepherd is back with his family," Mrs. Iverson says as she brings out a pile of board games.

There's Careers and Monopoly and a card game named Uno.

Amanda watches my face. "You choose, Justin," she says.

"Any one of them's fine by me," I say, looking at the games. "If you show me how to play," I add shyly.

The Iversons don't laugh or look at each other funny when I say that.

I hear Smokey sigh underneath the table. I move the tablecloth a little so I can get a better view. Smokey's lying there, with Isabelle and Isidor curled up next to him.

Acknowledgments

Special thanks to my best friend Viva Singer for reading the first draft of this manuscript and for hardly ever losing her patience with me when I phoned her at work to talk about dogs. Thanks also to Alanna Devine, acting executive director of the Montreal SPCA; dog trainer Robert Des Ruisseaux; and to security expert Gérard Farmer, all of whom took time out of their busy schedules to answer my questions about the work they do. Hats off and a big hug for Melanie Jeffs—my kind and clever editor—and to the team at Orca Book Publishers who help me tell my stories. And thanks, as always, to Mike and Alicia, the two big loves of my life.

Monique Polak is the popular author of many books for juveniles and teens, including *Finding Elmo* and *121 Express* in the Orca Currents series. Monique lives in Montreal, Quebec.